The Sapphire Princess Hunts for Treasure

THE JEWEL KINGDOM

The Sapphire Princess Hunts for Treasure

JAHNNA N. MALCOLM

Illustrations by Neal McPheeters

SCHOLASTIC INC.
NEW YORK TORONTO LONDON AUCKLAND SYDNEY

ISBN 0-590-11714-9

Text copyright © 1998 by Jahnna Beecham and Malcolm Hillgartner.
All rights reserved. Published by Scholastic Inc.
LITTLE APPLE PAPERBACKS is a trademark of Scholastic Inc.

12 11 10 9 8 7 6 5 4 3   8 9/9 0 1 2 3/0

Printed in the U.S.A.   40
First Scholastic printing, February 1998

To
Kathy and Bob
and their Royal Family:
Sara, Christine, and Peter

CONTENTS

The Sapphire Princess Hunts for Treasure

THE JEWEL KINGDOM

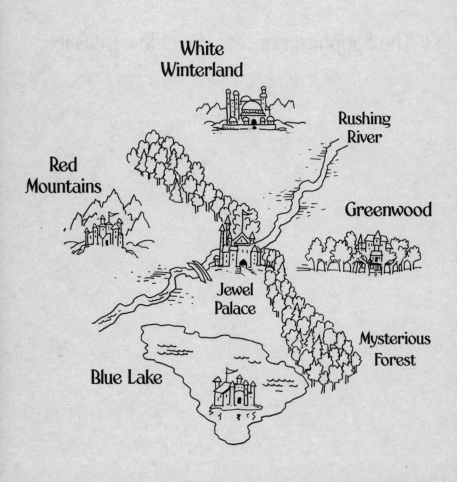

White
Winterland

Rushing
River

Red
Mountains

Greenwood

Jewel
Palace

Mysterious
Forest

Blue Lake

The Beautiful Blue Bottle

 "Princess Sabrina!"

Zazz the butterfly fluttered over the Sapphire Princess's throne. She pointed one wing at the blue-tiled pool in front of Sabrina. "Look!"

The princess leaned forward and looked in the water. "What is it?"

"Someone's coming," Titus, her palace

guard, answered. "They should use the front gate. Not your private pool."

The Sapphire Palace was built over Blue Lake. Water from the lake flowed into the pool through underwater gates.

"Don't be an old fuddy-duddy, Titus," Princess Sabrina said with a smile. "I love having visitors."

The princess smoothed out her blue chiffon gown. The dress was the color of the sky and matched her eyes perfectly. She straightened the silver crown that perched on top of her long blond hair. "Let them come!"

"If the princess is to have a visitor," Titus said, "that visitor should talk to me first!"

Titus was a Strider. His head looked like a big silver fish. He had large lips and big, droopy gray eyes. Green spikes traveled from the top of his head down his back. His hands and feet were webbed.

"Those are the rules!" the guard added.

"But Titus, that seems so formal," Sabrina said. "Why can't they just visit me?"

"Because I am your palace guard," he replied. "I am supposed to keep you safe."

Sabrina sighed. There were many things she loved about being the Sapphire Princess. But being guarded by a stick-in-the-mud was not one of them.

The princess had grown up with her three sisters in the Jewel Palace. Her parents, Queen Jemma and King Regal, had guards, too. But those guards were young, and fun. Sometimes Titus just seemed like a grumpy old man.

"Titus," Sabrina said, patting the guard's arm. "Thank you for being careful, but I don't really need to be watched so closely. After all, this is my home."

When Sabrina and her sisters were crowned the Jewel Princesses, each was given her own land to rule. Sabrina was given Blue Lake: a world of lily pads, weeping willows, and lake creatures.

Roxanne, the Ruby Princess, ruled the Red Mountains. Demetra, the Diamond Princess, had the White Winterland. Emily, the Emerald Princess, lived in the Greenwood.

Sabrina moved into her Sapphire Palace on the water and made friends with the creatures in Blue Lake.

"I feel very safe here," the princess said.

"A princess can never be too careful," Titus said. "Especially with visitors who won't use the front gate." He stared at the pool. Suddenly blue water shot in the air like a fountain.

"Look out!" Titus threw himself in front of the princess.

A tiny head popped out of the pool. It was a Water Sprite.

"Don't worry," the little Sprite giggled. "It's only me, Flotsam."

Titus put his hands on his hips. "You should have let us know you were coming. You frightened the princess."

Sabrina shook her finger at the guard. "That's not true, Titus. Now please move out of the way so I can speak to Flotsam."

Titus grumbled for a few more seconds. Then he shuffled off to stand beside her throne.

Flotsam rested her elbows on the side of the pool. She was a little girl with

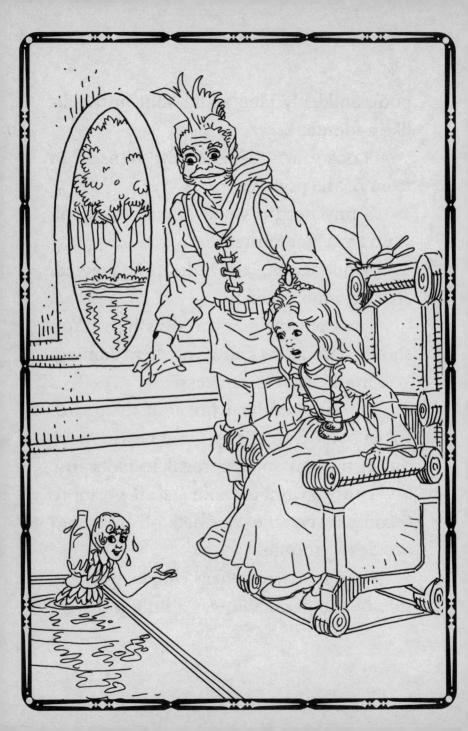

straw-colored hair and a tiny star on her forehead. Her skin was the color of pearls. She wore a swimsuit of green leaves.

"Princess, I was swimming at Bluebonnet Falls, and found something," she said in her high voice.

Sabrina knelt at the edge of the pool. "What is it?"

"A beautiful blue bottle." Flotsam pulled a bottle out of the water.

Titus sprang forward. "A blue bottle?" he repeated. "Let me see that!"

"No!" Flotsam ducked underwater. She swam away from the guard. "I want to give it to the princess myself!"

Sabrina followed Flotsam. "Of course you can give it to me, Flotsam. I would love to see it."

The Sprite held the blue bottle in the air. It seemed to glow.

"Oh, my," Sabrina gasped. "That is beautiful!"

The Sapphire Princess reached for the bottle. The instant she touched it, she heard a beautiful sound. Like two harp strings being plucked.

"Did you hear that?" Zazz asked, flitting closer to the princess. "I'm sure I heard music."

Sabrina didn't answer. She was too busy looking at the bottle. Now that she held it in her hands, the dark blue color had changed. She could see through the glass.

"There's something inside," Sabrina said, holding it up to the light.

Zazz circled around the bottle. "It

looks like a piece of paper with writing on it."

Sabrina turned the bottle and read the words aloud.

"This ancient map, if you unfold,
Will treasure show, wondrous to behold."

The princess looked up at her friends. Her eyes sparkled with glee.

"Flotsam has found a treasure map!"

A Treasure Hunt

 "Treasure!" a voice called from the throne room door. It was Gurt, the frog-faced Gilliwag. He hopped to join the circle around the princess.

Gurt's friend Shallow was right behind him. Shallow was the leader of the blue-skinned Nymphs. His green hair stuck out in tufts on top of his head. It matched his sea-green eyes.

"What kind of treasure?" Shallow asked.

"Jewels!" Zazz cried. "Lots of sparkling jewels!"

"Or coins," Flotsam squeaked. "Thousands of gold coins."

"It has to be something very rare and special," Sabrina added. "For that is what a treasure is."

"Let's go find it," Zazz said.

"A treasure hunt," Sabrina giggled. "What fun!"

"Open the bottle, Princess!" Zazz landed on the princess's shoulder. "Let's take a look at this map."

"Yes, open it, please!" Flotsam begged.

Sabrina turned the bottle over in her hand. There seemed to be no top or cap to it. "I don't know how to open it."

"Break the bottle!" Gurt croaked.

"Yes," Shallow said. "Break it."

"No, Princess!" Titus ordered loudly. "Do not break that bottle!"

Sabrina blinked at him in surprise. He had never shouted at her like that before. "Why not, Titus?"

The old Strider's face had turned from silver to a bright purple. "Because, well . . . because the blue bottle could shatter and you might hurt yourself," he sputtered.

"But how can I get the map?" Sabrina asked.

"You don't want that map," he said. "I'm sure it's not real. It's probably just a joke." He pointed to the Water Sprite. "A joke played by Flotsam. Or her brother Jetsam."

Flotsam's mouth dropped open. "That is not true. What a mean thing to say!"

"I have an idea," Sabrina said, trying to

keep Titus and Flotsam from arguing. "Let's tell the other creatures of Blue Lake about this bottle and map.

"But why do we have to tell the others?" Shallow the nymph asked.

"It would be fun for all of us to hunt for treasure together," Sabrina replied.

Flotsam groaned. "That's too many people. And there couldn't be that many places to hide a treasure."

Sabrina tucked the bottle into the pocket of her blue gown. Then she hurried to get her cape. "I'll be right back."

Sabrina grabbed her cape. She picked up the tiny blue purse that the wizard Gallivant had given her when she was crowned the Sapphire Princess.

The purse was filled with magic dust. The dust could make Sabrina fly. She never went anywhere without it.

When Sabrina returned to the throne room, it was empty. Except for Zazz, who zigzagged angrily around the room.

"Zazz!" Sabrina cried. "Where is everyone? Titus, Flotsam, Gurt, and Shallow?"

Zazz stopped in midair. "They went on the treasure hunt without us!"

Wait for Us!

The princess hopped into one of the leaf boats docked by her castle. She paddled toward the center of the lake, trying to find her friends.

Usually Zazz perched on the bow of the boat. Not today. She was too upset. The butterfly buzzed in little circles above Sabrina's head.

"I can't believe them!" Zazz said.

"Running off and leaving us like that. Some friends!"

"Zazz, calm down." Sabrina dipped her paddle into the water. "I think they were all just a little too excited."

"Too excited!" Zazz squeaked. "If you ask me, they're a little too greedy. They want that treasure for themselves."

"But I have the treasure map," Sabrina said. "They won't know where to find it."

Sabrina rowed the leaf boat around the first bend of Blue Lake. She floated through a clump of lily pads. Then her paddle hit something hard. "What was that?"

Zazz dipped down for a closer look. "A broken tree limb, Princess."

Sabrina frowned. There had been no storm to cause a tree to lose a limb.

"Watch out!" Zazz called. The boat

bumped against some floating bushes. The bushes were on their sides. Their muddy roots stuck out of the water.

"First the tree limb. And now those bushes," Sabrina said. "What is going on?"

As she spoke, several large clumps of dirt and two bunches of flowers drifted past the boat.

Zazz flew ahead of the boat. "Here's another tree limb. This one looks like it's from the Willow-that-Weeps."

"The Willow-that-Weeps!" Sabrina gasped. "Let's go see what's causing all this damage!"

Sabrina paddled into a narrow cove full of tall reeds. She pulled the boat up onto the green grass bordering the lake.

"Come on, Zazz," the princess called. "We have to hurry."

Sabrina and the butterfly followed a trail of trampled flowers and overturned rocks.

"Who would do this?" Sabrina asked as they hurried to the Willow-that-Weeps. "Who would ruin our beautiful home?"

"Treasure hunters," Zazz replied. "They want to find jewels and gold."

They reached the Willow-that-Weeps. The ground all around the tree was dotted with holes.

"Oh, Zazz," Sabrina murmured. "You're right. Our friends have been digging for treasure."

The Sapphire Princess quickly pushed dirt back into the holes. She started to fill the biggest hole, but stopped when she heard a voice.

"Wait, I'm down here," a little voice called.

Sabrina looked into the hole. "Flotsam? Is that you?"

"Yes, Princess," the Sprite said, miserably. "It is me."

"What happened?" Sabrina asked. "Did you fall in?"

"No!" Flotsam shook her head hard. "I was pushed!"

Break the Bottle!

Princess Sabrina pulled Flotsam out of the hole. The tiny Water Sprite's knee was bruised. The star on her forehead was smudged with dirt.

"Who do you think pushed you into that hole?" Sabrina asked. She helped Flotsam walk back to the lakeshore.

"I'm not really sure," Flotsam said.

"But it had to be one of the treasure hunters."

Zazz landed on a blade of grass beside the princess. "That means it was either Shallow, Titus, or Gurt."

"It wasn't me," a voice called from a clump of reeds. "I wanted the treasure but I would never hurt anyone."

"Who said that?" Sabrina asked, wading into the water.

A green froggy head slowly poked through the reeds. It was Gurt, the sad-eyed Gilliwag.

"When you left the throne room to get your cloak," Gurt said, "we all went a little crazy."

Sabrina nodded. "I thought that's what happened."

"Everyone was shouting, '*I'm* going to find the treasure,'" Gurt explained. He hung his head. "I feel very silly. And very ashamed of myself."

"You should!" Zazz said, circling the Gilliwag.

"Now, Zazz." Sabrina held out one finger for the butterfly to perch on. "Don't be so hard on Gurt." He's not the only one responsible for this mess."

Zazz folded two of her six legs in front of her. "That's right. Titus and Shallow are still on the loose, tearing up Blue Lake looking for that treasure."

Flotsam rubbed her bruised knee. "I wish you would read that map, Princess, and find the treasure before any more Blue Lake creatures hear about it and do what we did."

"With everyone running wild," Gurt added, "a lot of creatures could get hurt."

"Gurt has a point," Zazz said. "If you

find the treasure, then the others will stop hunting for it and be safe."

Sabrina had thought a treasure hunt would be fun for everyone. But it wasn't. It was actually becoming dangerous. Maybe she should just get it over with.

"All right," she said, pulling the blue bottle out of her dress pocket. "I guess the time has come to break this bottle."

The Sapphire Princess looked around for a large rock. She found one at the top of Blueberry Hill. Gurt, Flotsam, and Zazz stayed at the bottom of the hill.

Sabrina held the bottle up to the sunlight. Once more it glowed. "Break, bottle," she whispered. "Show us your map!"

The princess swung the bottle toward the rock. But someone caught hold of her arm. Then sand was tossed in the air.

For several seconds the Sapphire Princess couldn't see a thing.

When the air cleared, the princess cried, "Oh, no! Someone has stolen the blue bottle!"

Danger Falls

The blue bottle thief was getting away. The princess watched him run down the far side of Blueberry Hill. He wore a brown cape that he pulled across his face.

"Stop!" she cried. "Bring that back!"

The thief dove into some bushes at the bottom of the hill. Sabrina could just see the top of his head. It was green.

Green? she thought. *Shallow the Nymph has green hair. And he really wanted to find that treasure!*

"My lady!" Gurt called. "Are you all right?"

Sabrina shook the last bits of sand from her blond hair. "Yes. But the blue bottle is gone."

Zazz darted around Sabrina's head. "Sand was everywhere. I couldn't see you. I was so worried."

"I'm fine," Sabrina said to the butterfly. "Really I am."

"Who would do this?" Flotsam asked.

The princess pointed down the hill. The patch of green in the bushes was still there. "Shallow!"

Gurt narrowed his eyes. "I'll go get him, Princess."

"No," Sabrina said. "I should do it."

The princess looked Gurt and then Flotsam in the eye. "I want you to promise me you'll stay with Zazz. And not go off on another treasure hunt."

"We promise," Gurt and Flotsam said.

Sabrina smiled. "Good. Keep an eye out for Titus. I could really use him right now."

Suddenly the green-haired figure in the cape bolted out of the bushes.

"Princess!" Flotsam cried. "Shallow is getting away."

"Oh, no, he's not!" Sabrina ran down the hill after him. She chased Shallow through some birch trees. She called to him but he wouldn't stop.

If he runs much farther, she thought, *he'll reach the Rushing River.*

The Rushing River was on the border of her land. It moved very fast and was difficult to cross. No one ever tried to swim it.

The thief stayed in the trees until he reached the river's edge. Then, to Sabrina's dismay, he leaped into the Rushing River.

Sabrina saw a flash of green as he was swept away. "Oh, no!" she cried. "That water is too fast. And too cold!"

She ran along the riverbank, trying to keep the green-topped head in sight.

At the footbridge, she saw him grab for the stone supports.

"Help!" he cried. "Please!"

"I'm coming!" Sabrina shouted. But when she reached the bridge, the water had carried him to the other side.

Sabrina knew that an emergency leaf boat was hidden close by. She found it covered in weeds at the foot of the bridge.

"Hold on, Shallow!" Sabrina knocked

away the weeds and pushed the boat into the rushing water. "I'll save you!"

Sabrina nearly fell out of the boat, but she didn't care. One of her friends was in trouble. Sabrina was going to do anything in her power to help him.

The leaf boat banged against several sharp rocks. Then it whooshed under a fallen log. The princess kept her eyes glued on Shallow, who was far ahead.

If I don't catch Shallow soon, she worried, *he'll go over Danger Falls.*

The falls were very high. No one had ever gone over them and lived to tell about it.

At the bend in the river, Sabrina watched Shallow catch hold of a branch. He struggled and struggled. Then he finally pulled himself onto shore.

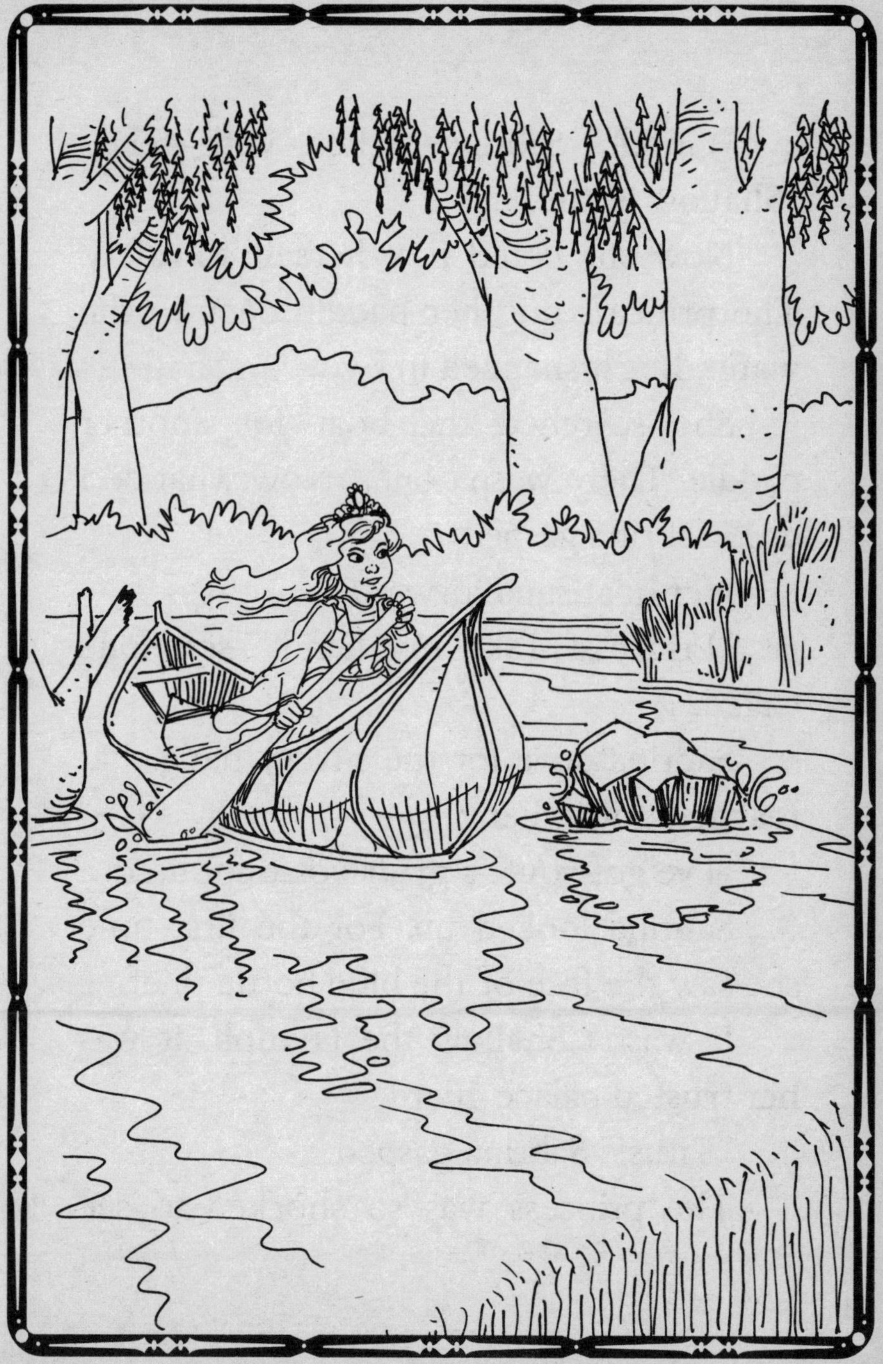

"Good!" Sabrina sighed with relief. "Shallow is safe."

Now she could row herself to safety. The princess dug her paddle deep in the water. But it snapped in two.

She searched the boat for another paddle. There wasn't one. "Now what do I do?" Sabrina gasped.

Her boat sped forward.

"Princess! Take my hand!" someone called.

Sabrina dove for the silvery hand that reached out to her.

"I've got you!" a gruff voice shouted.

Sabrina looked up. For the first time she saw the face of the blue bottle thief.

It wasn't Shallow the Nymph. It was her trusted palace guard.

"Titus!" Sabrina gasped.

The princess was so shocked to see

who the thief was that she let go of Titus's hand.

"My lady!" he cried as Sabrina's boat whisked her around the bend. The rest of his words were drowned out by a huge roaring sound.

The Sapphire Princess turned and froze.

There — as big as life, as loud as thunder — was Danger Falls!

Fly, Princess, Fly!

 Sabrina stared at the waterfall. It was like a magnet, pulling her to its edge.

The princess didn't know what to do. She couldn't row — her paddle was broken. She couldn't swim — the current was too fast. Sabrina looked up at the sky, trying to think.

"Of course!" she cried. "The only way out is to fly!"

The princess felt for the magic purse at her waist. She had only seconds to sprinkle its dust and say the magic words.

Sabrina's hands shook as she tossed the magic dust in the air.

"From water to air," she chanted over the roar of the water. *"Higher and higher, let me go!"*

Sabrina flew up, just as the tiny boat tumbled over Danger Falls.

"I made it!" the princess cried, spreading her arms out wide. "That was a close one."

Sabrina took a deep breath and tried to calm down. She let herself float through the air before she went back to look for Titus.

Finally, the Sapphire Princess turned and followed the Rushing River, looking for the guard. She found him sitting on a

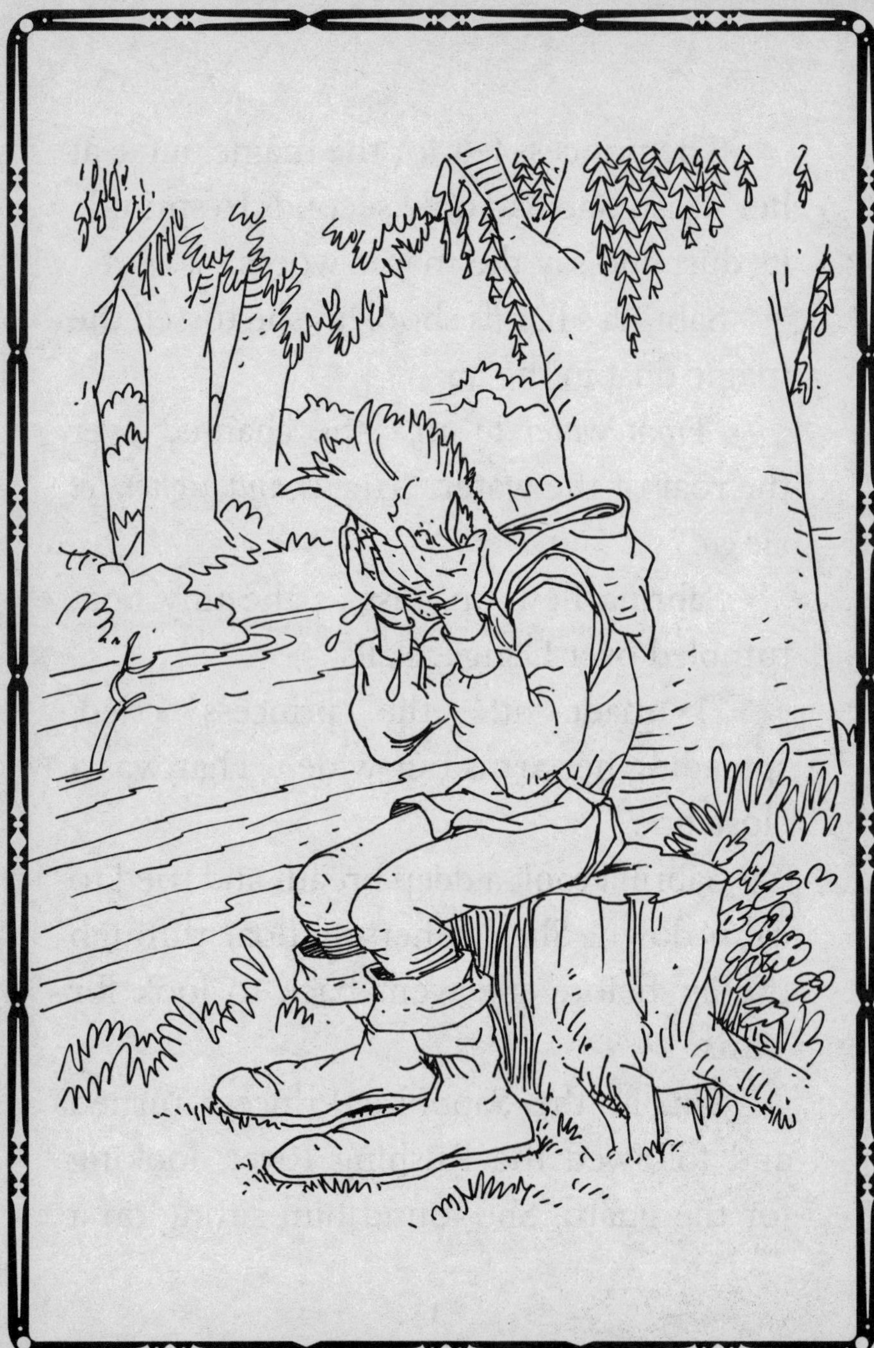

stump by the water. His cape was by his side, and his head was in his hands. Titus was crying.

Sabrina drifted gently to the ground beside him. "Titus, are you hurt?"

Titus looked up at the princess and gasped. He rubbed his eyes and looked again. "Princess? Is that really you?"

Sabrina nodded.

A smile lit his face. Titus jumped up and wrapped his arms around the princess. "You're alive! I was so afraid."

"So was I," she confessed.

"But I thought your boat went over Danger Falls." He wiped his tears with the back of his hand.

"The boat went over," Sabrina explained. "But I wasn't in it."

Titus dropped to one knee. "Oh, my princess. Can you ever forgive me?"

"Of course I can." Sabrina knelt next to Titus. "But tell me, Titus. Why did you steal the blue bottle?"

Titus was so ashamed he couldn't look at her. He stared at the ground. "I was afraid you didn't need me anymore. I wanted to show you that I could find the treasure."

"Oh, Titus," Sabrina said. "I do need you."

"Really?" he asked.

"Of course." Sabrina squeezed his hand. "You are my palace guard. But more important, you are my friend."

Sabrina thought this would make Titus happy. Instead, he burst into tears all over again.

"Oh, dear. Now why are you crying?"

Titus looked at her with his sad, droopy eyes. "Because I was looking for buried treasure and nearly destroyed the real treasure in my life — your friendship."

Sabrina handed Titus a lace handkerchief from her pocket. He took it and blew his nose hard. "Thank you, my lady."

The Sapphire Princess stood up. "What do you say we go home?"

"But what about the treasure?" Titus asked.

Sabrina waved one hand. "Let's forget about the whole thing."

"We can't forget about it, my lady," Titus whispered. "The blue bottle appears only once every hundred years."

Sabrina blinked in surprise. "How do you know that?"

"The story of the blue bottle and its treasure map has been passed down from generation to generation in my family,"

Titus explained. "My mother told me. Her mother told her. And *her* mother told her."

"But why haven't I heard about the blue bottle?" Sabrina asked. "And why didn't you tell us about the blue bottle when Flotsam found it?"

"Because it is a secret. A secret guarded by the Striders. If everyone knew that a treasure was here, they would destroy Blue Lake looking for it." He hung his head and added, "Like I nearly did."

Sabrina looked for the blue bottle. Titus didn't seem to have it. "Too bad the blue bottle is lost," she said.

"It's not lost." Titus reached into a leather bag at his waist. "I saved it. See?"

The guard held the bottle out to the princess.

This time, when her hand touched the glass, the bottle magically opened.

"Oh, my goodness!" Sabrina tipped the bottle, and the map slid into her hand.

Before she unrolled the map, the princess asked, "Titus, are you ready to find this treasure?"

Titus nodded. "Yes, but only if we find it together."

Sabrina carefully unrolled the map. There, marked with a big X, was the spot where the treasure was hidden.

Blackwater Bog

It was nearly dark when the princess and the guard returned to Blueberry Hill.

As promised, Zazz, Gurt, and Flotsam were still there. They had been joined by one other treasure hunter, Shallow the Nymph. He had spent the afternoon trying to climb out of a deep hole he had dug.

Princess Sabrina and Titus told the

story of their adventure at Danger Falls. Then Titus apologized to his friend for his sorry behavior.

After everyone shook hands and made up, the princess showed them the map. She pointed to the X located at the far side of Blue Lake. "That is where we'll find our treasure."

"But that's Blackwater Bog!" Zazz gasped. "That is a terrible place."

Shallow nodded. "Nothing is there. Just an old gray rock and a few lake weeds."

"That makes it the perfect place to hide a treasure," Gurt pointed out.

"But it's nearly dark," Zazz said, "and Blackwater Bog is a long way away."

"Zazz is right," the princess said. "The mudflats near the bog can be very dangerous. We might have trouble seeing them."

Titus cleared his throat. "I'd be happy

to light a torch, my lady, and lead the way."

Shallow the Nymph stepped up to the old guard. "I know a shortcut, Titus. We'll follow Lily Pad Lane."

"Good idea," Titus said.

Gurt joined the three of them. "I can croak a message to the other Gilliwags. They will help us cross the mudflats."

"And the Sprites will guide us to Blackwater Bog," Flotsam added.

"Then what are we waiting for?" Sabrina said. "Let's go!"

Titus and Shallow led the group down Lily Pad Lane and across the mudflats. The friends entertained each other by singing songs along the way.

The sun was setting as the Sapphire Princess and her friends arrived at Blackwater Bog.

It was a dark pool filled with dead

weeds and one huge gray rock. The shore was a long strip of dried mud. Nothing seemed to be growing there.

The friends had been happily singing only moments before. But now they were silent. They stood around the princess, staring at the black bog.

"It's even uglier than I remembered," Zazz finally said.

Princess Sabrina nodded. It was hard to imagine a treasure of any kind being in this awful place.

Gurt tried to wade through the lake weeds. "There's no treasure in here," he said. "The weeds are too thick."

"How about that rock?" Titus pointed his torch at the big gray rock in the middle of the bog. "Maybe it's under there."

Shallow snorted. "Not likely. Who could lift a rock that big?"

"How old did you say the bottle was?" Flotsam asked.

"A hundred," Titus said, staring at the bog.

"A lot could have happened in a hundred years," Zazz said. "Someone might have found that treasure long ago."

"That's true," Shallow agreed.

Sabrina sighed. She and her friends had gone through so much to find this treasure. And to have it all end like this was very disappointing.

"I hate to say this," Sabrina murmured, "but I think our treasure hunt is over."

Gurt nodded. "I think you are right, my lady. That bog is definitely empty."

"There's really nothing left for us to do but go home," the princess said sadly.

Zazz pointed one wing at the sky. "Luckily the moon is bright," she said, trying to cheer up the princess. "It will help light our way back to the Sapphire Palace."

The group turned to leave but Titus continued to stare at the bog.

"Come on, Titus," Sabrina called.

He shook his head stubbornly. "My mother, my grandmother, and my great-grandmother couldn't *all* be wrong. I have to stay."

Sabrina felt sorry for Titus. She couldn't leave him alone. He seemed too sad. "Then I'll stay with you," she said.

The princess turned to tell her friends to go on. But they weren't listening.

Their mouths were wide open. No one could speak. They could only point.

Something amazing was happening in Blackwater Bog.

The Treasure Is Found!

The black water was bubbling. The plants that looked like dead lake weeds were moving. They circled the big gray rock.

"Oh, my gosh!" Sabrina gasped as the rock began to split apart. "It isn't a rock at all. It's a flower!"

The petals unfolded, one by one. Each petal was a different shade of gold and silver. As the magnificent flower opened, gold stars shot into the air like fireworks.

The lake weeds were blooming, too. They circled the flower with all the colors of the rainbow.

Sabrina had never seen anything so beautiful in her entire life.

"The air!" Zazz cried. A wonderful smell filled the bog.

Flotsam and Shallow sighed. "Heaven!"

"Oh, Titus," Sabrina whispered. "The treasure isn't gold or jewels. It's this flower."

Titus chuckled and nodded. "Isn't it amazing?"

The shooting stars danced across the sky. They formed sparkling patterns above the great flower.

The princess and her friends "oohed" and "aahed" at the magical sight.

As they watched the flower, Sabrina had the feeling that she was not alone. She was right.

Birdlike creatures with long yellow legs and blue bodies lined the shore. They were the Storkz.

Sage, their leader, stood near Sabrina. A pair of gold-rimmed glasses perched on the tip of his beak.

"So it's true!" he whispered.

"Do you know about this flower?" Sabrina asked.

"When I was young, I heard a tale about a flower that bloomed once every hundred years," Sage replied. "But I thought it was just a story."

As they talked, more and more lake creatures arrived at Blackwater Bog. The sweet fragrance seemed to be drawing them to the flower.

Suddenly a huge gray head exploded out of the water. The creature had big yellow eyes and large pointed teeth.

"Oona!" Sabrina cried with delight. "You came, too."

"I wouldn't miss this for the world." Oona was the oldest creature in Blue Lake. She looked like a scary sea monster, but she was really very shy.

"I see you found the blue bottle," Oona said to Princess Sabrina.

"It appeared this morning at the base of Bluebonnet Falls," Sabrina said. "There was a map inside."

Oona nodded. "When this flower is ready to bloom, it releases the blue bottle."

Sabrina's eyes widened. "So the bottle came from the flower?"

Oona nodded again. "And it must be returned to the flower."

"Princess!" Zazz cried. "Word of this flower has spread throughout our land. Look, all of our people are here."

The shores of the bog were crowded with Nymphs, Gilliwags, Sprites, and Striders. They grinned and giggled. Sabrina giggled right along with them.

The princess and her people from Blue Lake would probably still be standing at Blackwater Bog watching that beautiful flower. But the moon began to set.

As soon as the moon's light dimmed, the flower petals started to fold together.

"My lady!" Titus grabbed Sabrina's hand. "The flower is closing."

"I know, Titus," she said wistfully. "But wasn't it beautiful?"

"Yes, yes," he sputtered. "But you can't let it close!"

Sabrina blinked her eyes in surprise. "I can't?"

"No. Oona said you have to put the map back in the bottle and return it to the flower. Remember?"

The bog water was beginning to bubble again. And the lake weeds were starting to move away from the flower.

"Hurry!" Titus cried. "Use your magic dust. Take that bottle to the flower."

Sabrina felt for her magic purse. "Titus, you are the guardian of the bottle. You should return it to the flower."

"But I can't fly," Titus sputtered.

Sabrina giggled. "Yes, you can. With me."

The princess tossed the magic dust over the guard and herself. She chanted, *"From water to air, let us fly!"*

Titus suddenly rose off the ground. "Whoa! What's happening?"

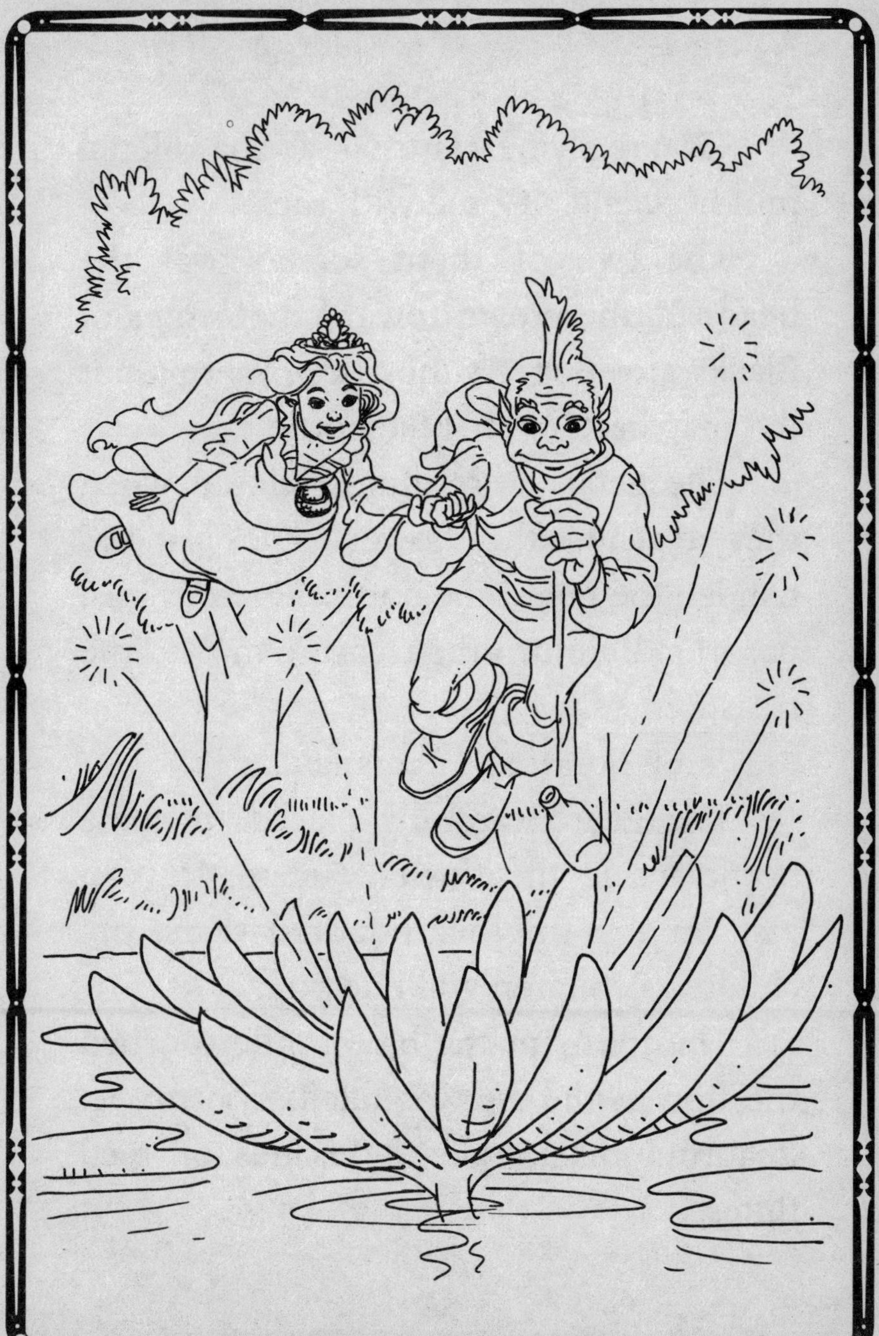

"You're flying, Titus!" Sabrina offered him her hand. "Come with me."

The two of them soared over the heads of the crowd toward the center of Blackwater Bog. As they flew, Sabrina put the map back in the blue bottle.

The petals were almost closed when they reached the flower. The princess handed the guard the bottle. "Here, Titus, my friend. Return the treasure map to the treasure."

"I am honored," Titus said.

The guard carefully placed the blue bottle inside the flower. "There let you rest. And in another hundred years, my children's children will find you."

The moment the blue bottle touched the flower, the air was filled with music. Beautiful music, like thousands of reed flutes.

Sabrina and Titus flew back to shore.

"This has been a great adventure," Sabrina said, smiling at her friends. "I want to thank every one of you for making it happen."

"Thank us?" Shallow repeated. "But what did we do?"

Sabrina pointed at the Water Sprite. "Flotsam brought me the blue bottle with the treasure map."

"Yes," Zazz cut in. "And everyone at the palace turned into greedy treasure hunters."

"We raced around our lake digging holes," Gurt said.

Flotsam pointed to her leg. "I hurt my knee."

"And I got stuck in the mud," Shallow added.

"And you nearly went over Danger

Falls trying to save me," Titus said to Sabrina.

"We did get off to a rocky start," the princess admitted. "But in the end, you all worked together. Shallow showed us a shortcut. Titus lit a torch and led the way. Gurt and the Gilliwags helped us to cross the mudflats. And the Sprites guided us into Blackwater Bog."

"We *did* work together," Flotsam squeaked. "And we found the greatest treasure of all."

"That's right, Flotsam," Sabrina said with a grin. "So, I truly want to thank you all for sharing this moment with me. It is one I will cherish for the rest of my life."

Sabrina joined hands with Flotsam, Gurt, and Shallow. Zazz perched on the princess's shoulder.

Together, they watched the silver-and-gold flower become an old gray rock again. And the lake plants turn back into dead weeds.

The flower was gone, but the music still filled the air. And happiness filled Princess Sabrina's heart.